Witchdaft

WRITTEN BY STEPHANIE SELBY

ILLUSTRATED BY ALEXANDRA SHAW

Copyright © Stephanie Selby 2025

Illustrations © Alexandra Shaw 2025

All rights reserved; no part of this publication may be reproduced or transmitted by any means without the prior permission of the author.

@stephanieselbyauthor

For my sisters,

who make me laugh the most.

Chapter One

If trees could talk, what tales would they tell? Spinning yarns on the breeze, humming through the leaves. With each creak they would speak - if indeed oaks spoke. If maples mumbled, damsons declared and poplars passed the time of day, then you may find yourself in Whispering Wood.

It had been named as such because not only did the trees speak to one another, but in fact they gabbed and gossiped about anybody that passed through their glade. On this particular occasion, they were talking about Prudence Hoodwinkle.

'Here she comes again wearing that ghastly cape. Is that what they're making them wear at Saint

Squiffler's Academy these days?'

'Who said that black was the new red?' observed a couple of nosey beeches.

Prudence Hoodwinkle was making her way through the wood to go and see her grandmother. Every Friday she would call via the village bakery after school and deliver her the goodies. What a sweet girl, you might

cared for fruit as a rule, but these looked too good to resist! She swiftly dropped her half-empty basket and a couple of raspberry jam tarts tumbled out into the dirt.

She groped at the tantalising berries and without a

moment's hesitation, pushed one after the other into her mouth. She lifted another to her lips but stopped after hearing a strange snuffling sound.

It got louder and louder, the snuffles turning into snorts. Prudence trembled with fear as she had been forewarned about the formidable creatures that resided deep in the wood. Prudence turned with dread to see what lurked behind her.

Thank goodness! The only things making a ruckus were a couple of chestnuts snorting and snickering at the fact that Prudence's cape had got caught in her knickers. She yanked out her cape wedgie and continued eating the juicy red jewels. Picking out the seeds from between her two front teeth, she felt a prickle from something hairy and possibly quite scary

on the back of her neck. She shrieked as the thing that was potentially about to eat her took hold of her school cape. She yanked at the bow that tied it round her neck and ran, screaming, as fast as her legs could carry her, all the way home. There sitting amongst the half-eaten strawberries was a plump, roly-poly pig - it had been gobbling up the crumbs that the girl had been leaving behind her. A shadow fell upon the curly tailed creature and a voice sounded from it saying, 'Marshall! What are you doing, you silly little pig?' There looking down through wiry half-moon spectacles was a little old woman dressed in an array of multi-coloured frills and patchwork. She looked scruffy and a little undone, but her face had a cheery disposition. She glared down at the greedy pig and lifted a finger to scold him further. 'You *know* you're on a diet - I thought we were in this together? I'm rather disappointed in you.'

She put both hands on her hips and began to turn on her heels when she stopped half pivot. The woman looked over her shoulder and her face creased into a sympathetic smile. 'Oh, Marshall, how can I be mad at you? Here, have a cookie.'

With her thumb and forefinger, as if flipping a coin, she flicked an invisible something into the air and out of nowhere appeared a small, chunky, chocolate chip

started to squirm out of already. 'I could just eat you up! But I won't because I had a big breakfast. Come on now, let's go, the girls will be here any minute. I've still got sour berry scones to make and the house is in a ghastly mess. Trot, trot!'

The old dear clicked her purple nail-polished fingers twice quickly and scuttled off towards a cosy looking cottage that sat under the shelter of a droopy willow tree.

12

Chapter Two

A scrumptiously sweet smell drifted through the air - but it wasn't coming from the lily of the valley that was growing nearby, nor was it Marshall who was covered in strawberry juice and the leftovers of Prudence's cream cakes. The delicious breeze that you could almost taste was coming from the cottage, which was completely homemade - not hand-built, you understand, but whipped up in the kitchen.

The entire house was chewable, crunchable, suckable, nibbleable and as far as Marshall was concerned, lickable, as he would drag his tongue up the jellybean pebble paved pathway. Cinder toffee brick walls held up the roof and huge hollowed out sticks of rock made up the guttering that read *'Made in Blackpool'* imprinted in blue lettering.

The windows were made of melted boiled sweets in all different colours, and the roof tiles of peanut butter brittle. The whole house glistened with a sugary glaze in the dusky evening light.

'Marshall! Will you stop that at once! What have I said about eating the house? Not for piggies, stick to your bowl!'

The woman's snouted friend unclamped his jaw from the gingerbread door, and proceeded to squeeze himself through a round hole that seemed to be Marshall's personalised pig flap. You could just about make out the teeth marks all the way around the hole where he had eaten his way in on a previous occasion.

centigrade and a molten consistency is achieved. Oven gloves and goggles must be worn at all times.' May's brow furrowed. 'Well there's no chance of getting *that* spell seeing as though *someone* ate the entire next page of the Volcano Cake recipe! As if it wasn't bad enough that you'd snaffled the sour berries I'd picked this morning! Are you trying to sabotage my girl's night, boy?'

She jerked her head over her shoulder at Marshall who was oblivious to her annoyance. He sat with a blank expression and above his head had appeared a hazy little cloud which contained images of dancing strawberries, half-eaten books and Prudence Hoodwinkle's hamper.

The irked old woman pulled a hairpin from the depths of her frizz and pricked the air over Marshall's head. The pig let out a little squeal as his thought bubble burst with a loud *BANG*!

May didn't even flinch and instead stamped on the floor and rapped her ladle on the side of the oven, splattering goo on the stone flags which Marshall mopped up immediately.

'Darren! We need a bit more throttle, love!' she called out.

WHOOOOOOOOOOOOOSSSHHHH!!!

The witch stumbled back as a furious fire rose up from the depths below the metal grating. The entire oven was enveloped in flames, making it glow a red the colour of May's lace-up boots.

'Give us a warning, would you?' May yelled as her hair sparked and smouldered from the blast. Marshall's snout hairs were scorched too, but he didn't seem to notice.

The mixture was now a dark orange colour and slightly crusting on the surface. 'Well, that looks lava-ly!' She chuckled at her own joke. Marshall didn't get it. 'Who needs an eruption spell when you've got a dragon in your cellar? I shouldn't imagine it'll make any difference to the recipe. Tell me what you think.' She dipped a teaspoon in the now lava-like mixture,

23

20

blew it to cool it a little and offered the spoon to the pig to lick, which he did with pure delight. Dunking another spoon into the pan, May gingerly licked the thick goo, spluttering as she did with small puffs of smoke escaping from her mouth.

'Goodness me!' she coughed, 'That'll put hairs on your chest!' No sooner had she said it, a few thick whiskers sprouted out of her chin and Marshall raised one of his eyebrows that had suddenly grown above his beady little eyes.

BOOM BOOM BOOM. Someone was at the door.

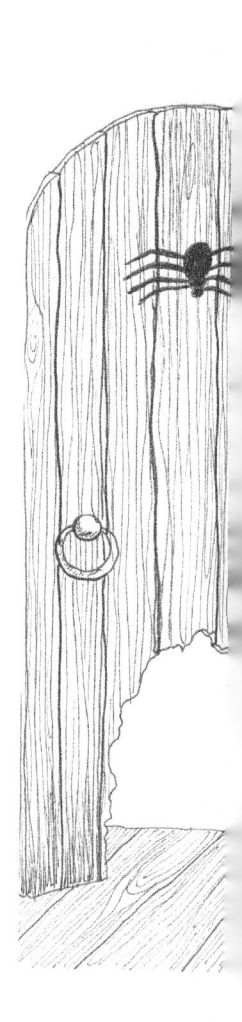

satisfaction that the little pig made echoed in the woman's nostrils. Her eyes were sunken in their sockets and decorated with heaps of mascara on the few lashes she had so that they looked like spiders' legs on her eyelids.

Aud lunged through to the kitchen where May was currently slopping the boiling batter into a cake tin. The spindly house caller hung her head over the tin to catch a whiff just before it got thrown into the back of the oven, the door of which May quickly secured shut with a broken broomstick.

She knocked twice on the oven door which must have been a signal for Darren to turn up the heat, and once again a roar of flames ignited from below and set the oven slightly aglow.

'Still using a Draga oven, are you?' Aud scoffed, 'You really should upgrade, sweetie. This thing's falling apart!'

'Oh, you know me, darling. I'm old school.' May winked. 'Also, dragon fire cooks in half the time!'

Whilst May busied herself, Aud started rearranging furniture in the living room. With each click of her bony fingers, the sofa and two armchairs which were once facing toward the fireplace were swivelling round to form a circle. 'Hmm, we're one chair short.' Aud scratched her chin in thought with a long gnarled fingernail. She eyeballed Marshall as if sizing him up to turn him into a footstool for the evening. Fortunately for the pig, she broke her plotting gaze and plonked herself on her favourite armchair. No one but Aud could sit in this chair; she had parked herself in it so often that she'd made an Aud-shaped indent in its cushions so no one else could possibly achieve any level of comfort in it.

'Oh, I'm sure they can all squish together, can't they, piggly? My feet, however, need a well-earned rest from the walk over here.' (Aud lived two minutes away.) She clicked her fingers once more and a line of peanuts appeared on the floor between Aud's feet and where Marshall was standing.

He caught the scent of the salty snacks that Aud had conjured and he began to munch them up, following the snaking line around the cottage's furnishings until he reached her feet which she promptly placed upon his hairy back. Marshall then stood in a daze as

'Looks absolutely…'

'…Delicious!'

'Always the hostess…'

'…With the most-ess!'

The twins giggled annoyingly as Lillian rolled her eyes.

'I don't think we've tried this one before have we, May?' Lillian reached out to cut a piece and as she lifted the knife, the cake started to rumble, making the whole cottage tremor. Crumbs sprinkled down from the ceiling like snow once again and Marshall stuck out his tongue to catch the crumb-fall.

The ladies didn't seem to be phased by the fact that they were experiencing a mini earthquake, or rather a cake-quake, which is what it was.

'Feels like a good one!' Aud remarked, clutching onto the arms of her chair. The spiders that had spun their webs in her hair were hanging on for their dear lives on account of the quake. Then at the crucial moment, the cake let out the most disappointing noise like when you let go of a balloon you've just blown up.
Pffffluuughhhhhffffffftttt.

The five women looked down at the cake which had deflated in the middle like a soufflé. Lillian was the first to speak, 'Was that supposed to happen?'

'I don't think so...' May said peering into the sunken cake hole, 'Maybe it was because I didn't use an eruption spell.' She cast a wicked glance at Marshall who had finished catching crumbs and was edging closer and closer to the caved-in cake. 'Ah well - I'm sure it will taste just the same! Help yourselves, ladies!'

A flurry of hands descended on the flattened cake, followed by a momentary chiming of forks on plates as every last morsel was eaten right up, most to Marshall's dismay.

May clicked her fingers and all the crockery and cutlery disappeared with a gentle *pop*! 'Ok, what are we making today, girls?'

At May's words, Rose and Violet started rifling around in their tiny matching handbags and at the same time each pulled out a pair of large knitting needles. Lillian pulled her pair out from the right sleeve of her green tweed jacket that matched her green tweed skirt. May reached down the neck of her

er bristly handlebar moustache that was twirling at

ends. The twins in turn had each grown a neat

e goatee beard in blue and pink to match their hair.

, bother! It must have been the cake! Marshall,

found you!' May cried out, although muffled

ugh her biker beard.

ian pointed at Aud, 'Look, you've started growing

---

dress and pulled out one knitting needle from each side of her bra like pistols from a holster, and Aud clicked her fingers and pulled one out of each gaping nostril. Lillian sighed in distaste.

'Shall we carry on…'

'…From last week?' chimed the twins.

'Indeed!' May agreed.

At the first touch of everyone's needles appeared an assortment of half-knit garments. May was knitting a new tangerine coloured poncho for herself, Lillian was finishing off a navy beret, the twins were working on matching lavender cardigans and Aud was weaving a black pashmina, complete with fashionable ladders and holes.

Of course, no one was knitting by hand, but allowing

the needles to click back and forth in mid-ai

helped them focus on the day's gossip.

As the needles ticked and tapped together a

ladies nattered away, Marshall let out a star

squeal.

'What's wrong, pudding?' May asked in ala

needles stopped clicking. Marshall stared a

The few stray hairs that had sprouted earlie

growing longer and longer, and more starte

appearing by the second.

'Merlin's beard!' Lillian proclaimed, mout

watching a fully fledged beard grow from

down to her belly.

'Uh oh…' the twins said in unison, lookin

The otherwise well-groomed lady was gro

a moustache too!'

Aud's brow furrowed to create deep cracks in her forehead. 'I didn't have any cake…' she said through clenched teeth.

'Oh.' Lillian went as pink as Rose's hair. 'Anyway, moving on… I don't know if you girls are having the same problem, but I'm having an awful lot of trouble with the local youngsters breaking into my garden lately! They've been trampling on my beautiful flowerbeds and pelting my bungalow with mud pies! It wouldn't be so bad if they weren't dipping into the pile of unicorn fertiliser to make them.' Lillian wrinkled her nose at the memory of the stench.

'Oh, how frightfully foul, Lily!' May gasped, hands covering her mouth. Her nail polish turned a shocking pink to match the witch's horror. 'I've been having the same problem - I caught a couple of them trying to chip out pieces of my peppermint rock guttering a couple of weeks ago - I've only just had it replaced, imported all the way from Blackpool! I tried to set Marshall on them both, but he's a bit slow these days, aren't you, petal?' Marshall wasn't listening and was now daydreaming about wallowing in Lillian's unicorn poo pile.

May continued, 'Even though I didn't get a very good look at them, I'm almost certain it was the Wretcher children. Now, what are their names...?'

Rose scratched at her new candy pink coloured goatee, 'Gert! And the boy is called...'

'...Floyd!' Violet remembered whilst taming her

ven branches out of each other and firs
ng and tearing the other trees down.
een torn out left, right and centre and all
d critters had started to take bets as to
ould 'TIMBER!' first. It took a good
hours to calm everything down and a few
hat to fix all the damage that had been
and Floyd's father was very highly
he Charlatan Community Council, so the
nswered for any of their wrongdoings.
ate' was never resolved and was
it down to a freak forest accident.
go smash up Warlock Bumbleton's
ch?' Floyd asked Gert as they were
gs with sticks in the wood's bubbling

bubblegum blue beard with a comb from her handbag.

'IMBECILES!' cried out Aud, which woke the little pig who had dozed off under her feet. 'How DARE they think that they can make a mockery of us!' The circle of bearded ladies nodded in agreement.

May stroked her wizard's beard in thought, which hadn't stopped growing and was now trailing on the floor. Marshall batted at it with his trotter. 'We'll have to keep an eye on those two. Three, in fact! I'm sure that little madam, Prudence Hoodwinkle, has had her nose in my strawberry patch this morning. The cheek of it! I've often seen the three of them lumbering around the village causing all kinds of trouble.'

'Well!' Lillian had heaved herself out of the sofa. 'If it carries on, I'll have to take some serious action and raise the issue at the next council meeting. Perhaps issue them with some DBOs!' *(Dreadful Behaviour Orders.)* 'That'll teach them!'

Aud blew a raspberry in disagreement. 'Like heck it will! They need teaching a lesson! Fight fire with fire, I say!'

'Well, we'll have to agree to disagree, Audrey, dear. Now, I must dash! I have to prepare for the bake sale tomorrow, I'm on the committee. I trust you're all prepared, ladies?'

Lillian looked down her moustached nose at May, 'Best stick to the recipes this time, hmm? We don't want any more hair-brained mistakes, do we?' May blushed. With a click of Lillian's fingers her knitting needles disappeared - with a second click, so did she.

Chapt

Gert and Floyd Wretcher w

behaved children in all of (

distress and disruption wh

terribly rude to whoever cr

Only recently they had bot

village because they had p

Whispering Wood. An elm

Floyd's unkempt appearan

cross that he found a spell

make all the trees turn rott

instead turned so nasty tha

each other!

Apple trees were throwing

bogs.

'Nah, he's put a protective charm around it since we did it last time,' Gert grunted in annoyance.

'What about if we try and chew off a bit more of May Marvel's candy cottage?'

'Duh? Don't you remember what happened last time,

you doofus? I still keep tripping over ever since she caught us last time and charmed my shoelaces to keep tying together! Plus, that stinkin' pig of hers almost ate Prudence - we could report her for that!'

'I've already tried.' Prudence had appeared behind them, which made them both jump and Floyd swore in surprise. One of the frogs gasped in shock.

'Blimey, Winkle! Where did you come from?'

'Yeah, you scared the snot outta me! You're askin' for a knuckle sandwich!' Gert protested, shaking a fist in Prudence's direction.

'Whatever,' Prudence muttered, kicking a mud clump into the bog. 'As I was saying, I tried telling Mummy about what that pig did to me, but she said it served me right for not going straight to my granny's. She also said that Ms Marvel is a well-respected resident of Charlatan, and she can't be making waves with her prescription of Snore Buns at stake.'

Mrs Hoodwinkle suffered from monthly bouts of werewolf wakefulness - a condition which gave her restless nights and spells of nocturnal behaviour. Symptoms included sleepwalking, occasionally chewing a pair of shoes, howling in her sleep and sometimes chasing the milkman down the road when it reached the early hours. Once the village apothecary master found Mrs Hoodwinkle rummaging through the bins in her nightie and hair rollers - she couldn't risk her reputation any longer.

Mrs Hoodwinkle soon got wind of May's sterling reputation for curative cakes and bakes, and the Snore

to really show off her skills.

The bake sale was held on the village green and May had arrived there early with Marshall to set up her stall.

'Come along, poppet!' May yelled to Marshall over her shoulder. 'The key to success is having a prime location!' She waddled along with baskets full of buns, cakes and loaves, and Marshall had a wicker picnic basket strapped to his back full of goodies. Entrusting Marshall with any kind of food would usually be asking for trouble, but to keep him distracted May had enchanted a donut to float *just* out of snout's reach so the greedy little familiar would be able to trot at her heels without wandering off. Within the hour, tables and stalls were being set up all

over the green with all sorts of delicious treats piled high on them. Even though the bake sale was held for a charitable cause (to fund the preservation of Whispering Wood) the competition was fierce and became only more ruthless with each year.

May had won Best Baker for nine years in a row and she was determined to make it an even ten. This year she hoped her Never-Go-Stale Scones would pip everyone else's bakes to the post but May was forever modest about her talents and would welcome a worthy competitor. She had also practised her gracious loser face for two full weeks.

'Morning, sweetie.' Aud had arrived to assist May on her stall. She was smoking her pipe and looked less than enthused with big dark bags under her eyes.

'Revoltingly early, isn't it?' Aud was a late riser and May assumed that perhaps she'd had one too many cockroach-tails the night before and was feeling a bit fragile.

Unlike May, making and baking weren't Aud's forte as her preferred subject at Saint Squiffler's was potions. Her Sweet-Talk Tonic was a potion she prided herself on the most - when slipped into a professor's morning coffee, all Aud would have to do was convince them that her assignments were worthy of top marks and she would waltz away with the highest grades for all her subjects.

Her unfailing formula had proved to be so effective that other students would pay top dollar for little vials of the stuff that Aud would hawk around the back of the broom shed. That was until Aud was rumbled by the school snitch, Cecelia Hoodwinkle. Aud was consequently expelled from Squiffler's and sent to work on a familiar farm on the outskirts of Charlatan.

gimmick.

One by one the villagers were drawn to May's stall like bees to a hive and soon a swarm was buzzing around the sweet treats. May was overwhelmed by this year's crowd and as she glanced around the green she noticed that customers for the other stalls were few and far between. Now, as May was a humble witch she knew that the other witches and warlocks were good contenders and so was suspicious of how quiet the surrounding stalls were. Even some of the other vendors had come over to buy her bakes.

She turned to Aud to express her concern and her mouth dropped open. Her friend was wired and practically fizzing with energy, dealing cash hand over fist whilst engulfing the crowd in a cloud of

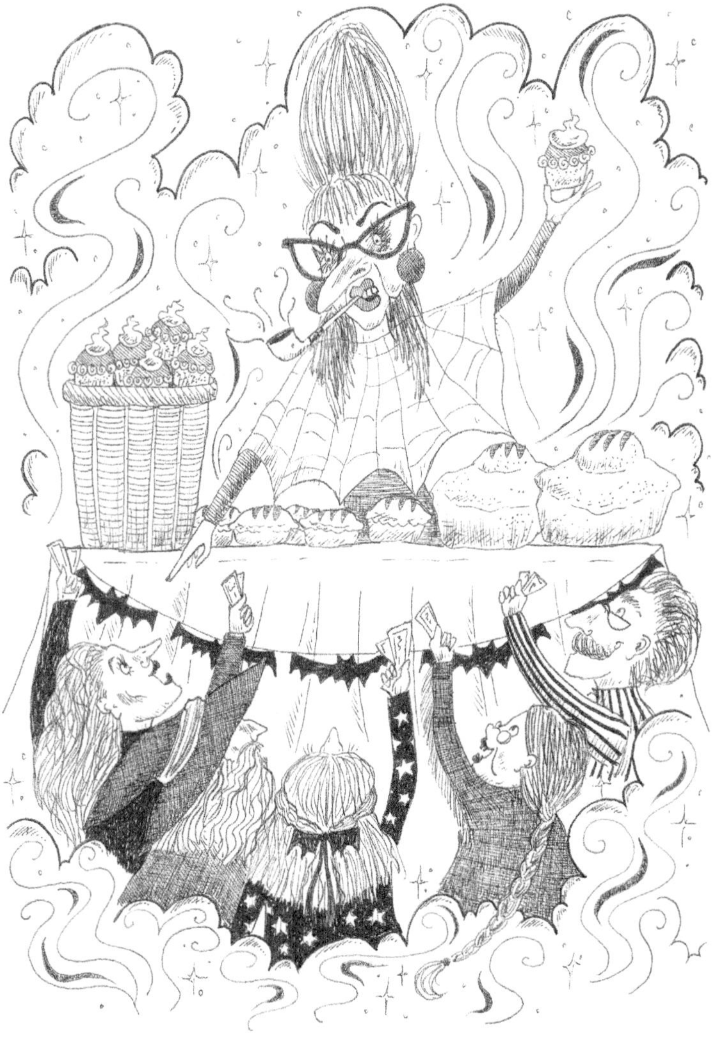

green pipe smoke.

She was bartering with customers like a cattle auctioneer. You could barely tell what she was saying as she was speaking so fast with the pipe clamped in her teeth. The crowd seemed to be in a trance handing their money over to Aud.

'Three of your Snore Buns, please!' a small, oddly dressed woman ordered over the table waving a coin purse full of change at Aud.

'Would you like a few Maca-Runes thrown in for half the price?' Aud squinted through the smoke at the customer who was wearing sunglasses and a headscarf tied under her chin. She waved the green smog away to get a better look.

With a nervous voice the character said, 'Er, no thank

you! Just the Snore Buns, dear…er, Madam!' She looked uncomfortable and fumbled around in her purse, dropping change all over the grass by her shoes that were two sizes too big.

In fact, every element of this person's outfit was particularly ill-fitting. Her stockings had a few holes in and were baggy and wrinkling around her ankles and her jumper was too long in the sleeves and kept slipping down over her hands. It looked like she'd put on a load of old clothes from the lost and found box at The Rusty Cauldron Rest Home.

Aud scowled at the weird little woman and corrected her immediately, 'It's Mademoiselle, I'll have you know! Madam makes me sound like an old woman!'

Marshall glanced at May in confusion as Aud was

mortal danger.

He shrugged his pork shoulders and continued to follow the path of crumbs. They wound in, under and out of the numerous tables until Marshall was on the outskirts of the village green.

The trail had come to an end but the pig could still smell the sweet scent of something tasty in the air. He snuffled around in the perfectly pruned shrubberies that lined the green. To Marshall's disbelief, a Snore Bun had tumbled out of somebody's hamper and into the borders. Without a moment's thought of the consequences, the pig pounced on the bun and swallowed it down in two bites. He let out an oink of satisfaction and slumped in a heap in the shade away from all the excitement.

Marshall could feel himself slipping into a slumber until all that he could hear was the faint sound of his own snoring. His eyelids sank shut and he started to dream of mud pies with flies on the side…

Chapter Six

'Marshall? Maaarshaaaall?!' May trilled over the green where people were now packing up their stalls. 'Where has he got to, the silly swine?'

There wasn't that much to pack up at May's table as Aud had managed to sell every single item - she had even cleared out the emergency hamper that May had prepared just in case Marshall managed to get his chops around some of the goods during the day. In fact, Marshall had remained quite restrained for most of the afternoon, which was rather unusual.

Aud clicked her fingers and her favourite armchair from May's living room appeared behind her. She fell back into its grooves and counted through the

Page 65

her eyes had glazed over slightly as she
a smile, 'Of course, you're right, it's all
of…' May suddenly spluttered and
the fumes that had started to float away

E you try to bamboozle me, Audrey
Wigglebottom!' May bellowed.
at May in repulsion - she was never
by her full given name. In fact, May was
e only one still alive who knew it. Aud
how much she'd upset her best friend and
ly apologised, 'Sorry, sweetie, I only
to win.'
n't find out who'd succeeded as Best
the Charlatan Community Council had

Page 62

earnings her and May had made that afternoon. May bustled around her, folding up tablecloths and packing away hampers with clicks of her fingers. May peered over her half-moons around the green, a look of concern crinkled her forehead.
Oh, don't worry, May. He'll turn up. He probably got bored once we started to sell out and trotted off home. Boy, oh boy, did we clean up today!' Aud scoffed,

fanning herself with a fat wad of notes. As she leant back in the chair, a little bottle slipped out of her pocket and tinkled to the ground.

Inside the bottle were dregs of a luminescent green liquid which May immediately recognised from their school days. As soon as it hit the floor Aud's eyeballs almost popped out of her head in panic. 'That's not mine!' Aud lied through the gaps between her teeth. May's lips could not have pursed any smaller as she glowered at her guilty friend. May shouldn't have been surprised as Aud had tried to pull the wool over her eyes on countless occasions over the years.

'Trickery! BETRAYAL!' May wailed, pointing a sparkly red fingernail in rage between Aud's eyes. 'I specifically said no potions of any kind! When I win-

I mean, *if* I win Best Baker I

title knowing we swindled e

Aud rolled her eyes as May

in disgrace.

Aud picked up the small via

chair and tapped the remaini

pipe that she'd fished out of

flicked her thumb on her fin

flint, and a flame appeared

She puffed on the pipe agair

green cloud into May's face

could manage, she calmly s

there's nothing wrong with

all in the spirit of competiti

May lifted her head from he

conferred and it was announced in the weekly newsletter in a few days.

Both May and Aud made their way home in awkward silence, whilst the empty hampers floated behind them. As they passed through Whispering Wood, a mass of maples couldn't help but remark on the two witches.

'Looks like *someone's* getting the silent treatment, wouldn't you say?' one said.

'You could cut that tension with a knife!' snarked the other. Aud shot the trees a look so diabolical that their leaves instantly shrivelled up and fell to the ground. They finally reached May's cottage but something was amiss, in that everything in the cottage was untouched. The gingerbread patch job that May had baked to fill in Marshall's pig flap was still intact and hadn't even been nibbled at by her familiar friend. May presumed that the little pig had trotted off to see what else he could scoff back at home.

However, the jellybean pebble pathway wasn't sticky underfoot where Marshall usually licks it and the Blackpool rock guttering wasn't glossy with pig saliva either. May turned to face Aud with a look of pure terror and said, 'I think Marshall's gone missing!'

Chapter Seven

Marshall started to stir from what he thought was one of the most marvellous afternoon naps he'd ever had. Usually when he woke from his two o'clock snooze, the delectable smell of whatever May was cooking would waft under his nose and rouse him like smelling salts.

Today, however, there were no familiar smells at all. No smell of cakes or delicious home cooking, but of tacky perfume, cherries and a hint of old cheese. He opened his right eye just a fraction enough to get an idea of where he was. He figured that he was in somebody's bedroom. After blinking both eyes open he saw a pile of clothes in a heap next to where he

---

frilly pink bonnet, with matching dress

tion from his tongue was in fact cherry gloss.

ned in despair. He hated bonnets. He'd le to carry them off. However he loved

was lying.

Amongst the jumble of clothes was a jumper, a headscarf, and just one battered looking loafer where the smell of old cheese was coming from.

The room was decorated in every shade of pink and was either fluffy or covered in glitter. Fuschia bedding, candy floss cushions, flamingo curtains and rose petal wardrobes.

The gleam from the amount of sequins was making Marshall go dizzy - either that or he'd missed a meal. He then heard the sound of a girl who he guessed was the owner of this bedroom.

'No, no, no! You've spelt it all wrong!' the girl whined. 'We want the old bag to actually be able to read the letter!'

Marshall sensed someth[ing and pricked his] ears up to hear two othe[r voices.]

'Whatever, Winkle,' a b[oy's voice said, 'it] looks real professional -[just like a proper kidnapper.]

'You mean, *pig*napper?'

Both the boy and girl ca[ckled, catching their] breaths.

'Good one, Gert,' snick[ered the boy.]

'Thanks, bro,' the girl r[eplied.]

Marshall was beginning [to realise these two] were up to no good. He [sniffed the air and] snuffled around the app[roaching a mirror. At the] sight of himself in the [mirror, Marshall] squealed in alarm as he [saw what they] had done to him. He wa[s covered]

underneath [...] and bloome[d ...]

To top off th[e ...] gruesome a[ct ...] they had als[o ...] painted his [...] cheeks with [...] blusher and [...] his lips with [...] sticky red [...] goo, which o[n ...] further inspe[ction was ...] flavoured lip[...]

Marshall gro[aned, he had] never been a [...]

cherries, so the lipgloss would have to put him on until tea time.

Suddenly, the three culprits barged through the door.

'Finally, the lazy pig's awake!' said Floyd, who was a brutish looking lad with a face like a bulldog chewing a wasp. His expression was in a scrunched up frown like someone had punched him in the face, if his face was made out of dough.

Marshall felt affronted by the name calling, but then remembered he was in fact, a pig.

'How many Snore Buns did you give him, Prudes?' asked a sullen girl who was spectacularly pale and dirty looking at the same time.

'Enough. And we've got a spare just in case he doesn't co-operate.' Prudence glared down at the pig who had now licked his lips clean of cherry lipgloss and was edging nearer to the old cheesy shoe. He hadn't eaten in what he thought was at least an hour and he was ravenous. He was considering causing a commotion just to be in with a chance of getting that spare Snore Bun.

'So, is everyone clear on the plan?' Prudence asked her cronies. Her accomplices looked blank, so she gathered it was a unanimous yes. 'Good! Right, all we need is a photograph of porky here to prove he's our hostage and we'll send it along with the letter. You got the camera, Gert?'

Grubby looking Gert took off her rucksack and rummaged around inside it to find an old-fashioned instant camera. 'Swiped this piece of junk from my grandpa's house,' she boasted through the cavities in her teeth. She held it to her eye and said, 'Say cheese, Sir Snorts-a-Lot!' Floyd roared at his sister's joke. Marshall however, had produced a thought bubble which had appeared over his head at the sound of the word cheese and was daydreaming of devouring a whole wheel of stilton.

all over Whispering Wood and throughout the village! You would have thought *someone* would have seen *somebody* take him - he's not exactly hard to miss!' May was thumbing through the remaining missing posters in desperation. 'Where else can we put them?' She had used the best picture of Marshall she could find, and in his best suit no less, which was incidentally just a lone black bow tie. The photo was taken at May's retirement party at Charlatan Town Hall which the CCC had organised in thanks for May's contribution to the community for one hundred years of business. Unfortunately, Marshall wasn't smiling for the photo because the picture was taken before they opened the buffet and so he looked terribly disgruntled.

Aud chirped up from her chair. 'Can't you find something in that recipe book of yours that could help find him, May? What good is it being a witch if you can't use magic when you really need it?'

'No, darling, I can't think of a thing! I just don't understand why someone would take him? Oooohhh dear, oh dear!' May buried her head into the sofa and began to sob.

'For goodness sake, May, get a grip! We'll find him! Did you not get him chipped or anything when you adopted him as a familiar?' Aud was now standing over May, hands on her bony hips.

'Nooooo!' May howled. 'They only chip cats, rats, bats and gnats!'

'Gnats?' Aud looked puzzled.

'They never chip pigs. They're too dependent on their food bowls! Why else do you think I made my house so delicious? It's practically a homing device for Marshall. He always follows his snout straight to it. He could be blind and still smell his way home!'

There was a silence that lasted about three and a half seconds before May sat bolt upright and a lightbulb appeared above her head.

'Merlin's moccasins, of course! Tracker Snacks! I could bake up a batch and sniff out his trail!'

'Daaaaaaaarren!' Aud boomed in the direction of the Draga, 'Fire it up! We've got some cookies to bake!'

In approximately forty-three minutes May had whipped up a dozen Tracker Snacks - chocolate chipped to boost their GPS signal.

May levitated one in the air with a wave of her hand and it hovered just under Aud's nose hairs. 'You eat the cookie, Audy, and I'll keep a clear head and make notes.'

Aud narrowed her eyes at May. 'A clear head? Why? What's it going to do to me?'

'Well, I may have overdone it on the dog slobber so it might give you more canine tendencies than normal, but it should be fine.'

'Dog sl-?!' But before Aud could utter another syllable, May had clicked her fingers and the cookie had shot straight into Aud's mouth.

The moment the Tracker Snack had passed Aud's wizened lips her mouth began to sag. Her face appeared as though it was melting - her jowls began to droop lower and lower until they dangled just above her shoulders. May tried to conceal the look of horror that was passing across her face as Aud's nose began to widen and her nostrils flared.

'What? Do I look different?' Aud asked, as she grew a few extra whiskers.

As far as May was aware, the spell was only supposed to give you a bloodhound's sense of smell with perhaps a bit of a wet nose, but it looked like the cookies had gone the whole hog… or whole dog.

'Right! No time like the present!' May ignored Aud's question and flung open the gingerbread door in an eagerness to find her familiar and to encourage Aud to leave the house and avoid looking in the mirror.

Chapter Nine

Aud had never moved so fast in her life. As soon as May opened the front door, Aud was out like a shot and had cocked her leg on the drooping willow tree.

'Aud, no!' May cried out and clapped her hands over her face. 'Get a hold of yourself, sweetie!'

Aud looked mortified and immediately stood upright and straightened up her pashmina. 'So sorry, I have no idea why I did that.' Aud's cheekbones went a faint pink, the only flush of colour May had ever recalled seeing her friend's face have aside from the usual gaunt grey. 'Grey is the new suntan, darling,' Aud would say.

Aud cleared her throat as a signal that she had

regained her usual surly composure. 'Onward!' she barked.

May followed hesitantly just in case Aud started chasing squirrels or dragging her bum along the floor. They continued on through Whispering Wood, careful not to get in ear shot of the trees that were passing comment on the strings of drool that Aud was producing from her jowls.

'Have you picked up anything at all, Audy?' May enquired behind her friend who was now crawling on her hands and knobbly knees, dragging her nose along the floor and up the odd tree trunk.

'I'm getting…a hint of…brie? No…camembert!' Aud inhaled deeply which sucked the tree's leaves and May's hair in the direction of Aud's nostrils like a vacuum.

A particularly perturbed plum tree loomed down on Aud. 'Mmmhmm?' the tree mumbled, unimpressed. 'Honey, you try'na say my sweet fruits smell like old cheese?' The tree was clearly offended, its lower branches bent and resting on its tree hips.

May tried to appeal to the plum tree's better nature, 'I'm so sorry about my friend, but you wouldn't have happened to see a lost pig wandering through the woods, I don't suppose?'

The tree's boughs furrowed and said, 'Who d'ya think I am, neighbourhood watch? You're barkin' up the wrong tree, lady! Get outta here!'

They hurried further along the pathway as May knew better than to ask anything of the wood. All they did was spread rumours and if you listened to them you'd end up chasing your tail. Speaking of tails, May had caught sight of something wiggling at Aud's rear end under her clothes.

Neglecting the fact that Aud had potentially grown a fully functioning tail, May figured that a wagging tail meant her friend was on to something. 'What is it, sweetie? Have you found something? Is it good news?'

'I don't know…I just feel… excited! Happy! The smell of something is pulling me along like a magnet!' Aud galloped along, picking up speed towards a clearing in the forest.

May's heart soared at the thought of squeezing Marshall's chubby cheeks again. But when they reached the clearing, there was nothing but a stinking muddy bog which was steaming in the sunshine. The smell was almost unbearable. May's face crumpled with disappointment and disgust, whereas Aud's eyes lit up and she flew off in the direction of the bog.

'Don't you even think about it, Aud! Bad girl! Here! I say, come here!' But it seemed that Aud had lost all control. She paused for a moment, looking May straight in the eye briefly, then plunged herself face first into the bog and proceeded to roll around in it. She only stopped when she heard muffled spluttering and choking coming from underneath her.

'Oi! You trying to make me croak before my time?' May lunged to grab Aud to hoist her out of the mud. Cemented into the sludge was a skinny frog looking rather roughed up.

'Can't a guy have a mud bath in peace these days? If I'm not being sat on, I'm being poked at with sticks by young punks!'

By now, the effects of the Tracker Snacks had begun to wear off and Aud suddenly became very self-aware of her behaviour. Her human nose had now caught a whiff of what she was just rolling in and her face scrunched up so much that her features were buried by her wrinkles.

'Satan's socks! What is that awful *stench*?' Aud looked down at herself covered in bog mud. 'Why does it taste like I've been chewing on a stick? And there's something else I can't quite lay my tastebuds on…'

May decided not to tell Aud that she had started to tuck into Lillian's fertiliser heap as they passed by her house and so changed the subject.

May stooped down to talk to the frog who was straining to sit up and suck himself out the mud.

'I'm so sorry! I must excuse my friend, she's not really feeling herself today.' They both turned to look at Aud who had clicked herself clean and was now blowing the mud out of her nose.

'What is your name, Sir?' May politely addressed the frog.

'The name's Gareth. Although you may know me by another name…The Watchdog.'

'You mean, Gareth the grass?' Aud guffawed. She knew exactly who he was. He was the biggest muckraker in town! If anything happened in Charlatan, 'Gareth the grass' knew about it, and would proceed to tell everybody. He supplied Whispering Wood with most of its material!

'I ain't no snitch! I just know a lot of stuff about a lot of things. You'd be shocked with the dirt I have on people. I suppose you could say I'm kind of a big deal around here.' Sounds of the swamp gurgled and chirped in awkwardness.

Aud rolled her eyes so you could hear them rattling in their sockets. 'If you say so, Watch Frog. So what can you tell us about our missing pig, oh wise and warty one?'

The frog shot daggers at Aud. 'Yeah, I might know something about a missing pig…but information doesn't come for free, you know. This ain't my first rodeo, ladies.'

Aud was about to launch at the slimy creature in temper before May quickly interjected. 'What is it that you want? More mud? A foot spa? What could a frog possibly need?' May asked.

The frog looked sheepish suddenly, if that's even possible. 'I want…a seduction spell.'

Aud pinched her lips together to stop herself from laughing. The frog didn't seem to notice. He appeared to have floated off in a daydream. 'I want to ask Minnie Mucus out on a date. She's the most amazing amphibian I've ever laid eyes on.'

Before Gareth could swoon any sicklier, May shook his tiny webbed hand and said, 'Ok, lover boy, you've got yourself a deal. This should do the trick!'

May clicked her fingers and a small vial filled with a deep pink liquid appeared out of thin air, hovering just out of the frog's reach.

Mesmerised by the bottle, pink reflected in the shine of his eyeballs, he stuttered, 'And this will make her knees weak for me?'

May held up her hand to hush her friend before Aud had chance to make a mocking remark. 'She'll be like a moth to a flame! Or a frog to a bog, as it were. Of course, you'll have to put most of the effort in yourself - this cologne will merely catch her interest - the rest is up to you.'

'Yeah, yeah, lay it on me, lady!'

May snatched at the floating vial, 'First, tell me what you know, Mr Watchdog.'

'Fine, fine. So here's what I heard,' the frog began. 'A couple of days ago three Squifflers were hanging around my bog. They were yapping on about teaching some old hag a lesson.'

'Hag?! Did they have mud in their eyes, the little

rats!' Aud started to steam from her ears.

May continued, 'Anything else, Mr...er, Dog?'

'Yeah, now you mention it. They said they were going to hatch their plan at a bake sale a couple of days ago...and I'm sure they mentioned a pig. Or maybe one of them just looked like a pig. Horrid little trolls they were - especially one of the girls.' He shuddered at the thought.

'Can you tell me what they looked like?' May appealed to the frog. 'Anything else at all would be tremendously helpful.'

'Like any bad apples, obviously! Sour faced, with a stinking attitude! One of them looked like Goldilocks gone wrong. The other two looked quite similar - nasty little toe-rags. They both stink up my bog on a regular basis.' The frog began to scoop up mud and rub it into his armpits, before flopping back into the bog.

May turned slowly to Aud who was practically frothing with rage. 'Hoodwinkle…' she growled.

Chapter Ten

'We should've known!' Aud stomped back and forth through May's living room in her muddy wellingtons, her eyes wild with mania. May tried to ignore the mess Aud was making, as there were more pressing matters at hand. 'I knew it wasn't the end of Cecelia Hoodwinkle's reign of villainy!'

Prudence was Cecil and Cecelia Hoodwinkle's only daughter, and it seemed that the rotten, worm-ridden apple didn't fall far from the tree when Prudence was born. According to Aud, Cecelia was her sworn enemy after she got Aud expelled from Saint Squiffler's.

Whenever Aud and Cecelia would cross paths in

Charlatan, black menacing clouds would hang heavy above the town in accordance with Aud's wrath, and everybody who was in the area would scatter and take cover before the storm exploded. It was very inconvenient and even more so on market day, so they avoided the town centre at peak times.

Even though May wasn't the biggest fan of Cecelia Hoodwinkle, she couldn't help but feel that Aud tended to overreact. After all, Aud used to cheat in every subject except potions, and she frequently gave Cecelia a Wednesday wedgie, so she kind of had it coming.

But the beef between Cecelia and Aud wasn't important right now, it was the pork that May was more concerned about. May snapped her fingers to break Aud out of her nostalgic funk. 'It's time to call the girls, don't you think, sweetie?'

The knitting coven had gathered in May's front room after she summoned them via text message - not very mystical, but they had to keep up with the modern age. Their knitting needles had been conjured and were clicking in unison with revenge.

'It's time these snot-faced Squifflers learnt a lesson!' Aud snarled as she thumped her fist on the arm of her chair which created a cloud of dust.

Lillian held up her hand in protest, 'Are you sure we shouldn't report the little beasts instead? Their parents are on the council, you know.'

'That's precisely why we shouldn't!' Aud argued. 'They'll just get away with it! Cecelia Hoodwinkle will cover anything up to save that prissy reputation of hers.'

Lillian looked uneasy. She always did things by the book, and the thought of taking matters into her own hands and going against the rules was enough to give her a nervous breakdown.

Rose and Violet were quite the agreeable types and so were nodding along enthusiastically with what anyone said. In fact, it had been a while since either of them had said anything so Rose chirped up, 'Time to teach them some…'

There was a silence whilst everyone waited for Violet to finish Rose's sentence, like she usually did. May peered over her glasses at Violet, 'Well?' she asked on behalf of the room.

'Errr…two in the bush? Flock together? Eggs in one basket? Two pounds of butter? Thursday?' Violet looked bewildered.

Rose rolled her eyes in despair. 'She hasn't been able to hear a thing since she grew that beard. She must have grown some hair in her ears too!' Violet continued to look vacant.

'Anyway!' May continued, 'These hoodlums have gone too far this time! Come on now, girls! We've got no time to fix dropped stitches! Knit like your pension depends on it!'

The knitting needles clicked even more furiously so that smoke started to appear due to the friction. Aud started to recite a spell…

'Knitta knitta net to hook 'em, spice 'em nice before

you cook 'em!'

Aud shrieked at the top of her lungs and cackled in a vengeful frenzy. Lillian looked mortified upon hearing the spell which made Aud roar even more raucously. 'I'm only kidding, you old goose!' she jovially slapped Lillian on the back which almost caused her dentures to come loose. This made Rose and Violet explode in fits of giggles which also made May unable to stifle hers in her bosom any longer. Before long, all the witches were cackling like the old days, but the smoke from the knitting needles started to make them cough so Rose had to pass around her inhaler.

The plan was in motion.

Chapter Eleven

The girls had spent all night planning and plotting Marshall's rescue. May knew that Cecelia would be due another batch of Snore Buns and so would deliver them to her house personally.

Once they had gained entry, they wouldn't have long to find out where Marshall was being held captive, so May had to do her best to distract Prudence's mother long enough for Aud to swipe their piggy friend unnoticed.

'Are you alright in there, darling?' May was standing outside the Hoodwinkle household with her shopping caddy by her side, talking in the direction of its contents. In amongst a fresh batch of Snore Buns was

103

Aud with what looked like a large fishing net.

You wouldn't expect Aud to be particularly flexible with her long gangly limbs, and you'd be right. May's shopping caddy was enchanted to fit an enormous amount inside it - including an old, cantankerous and sharply-built witch.

'Just peachy…' Aud said through gritted teeth. 'It may be spacey in here, but it sure smells a bit funky! What do you keep in here?'

May recalled letting Marshall clamber inside when his little trotters got tired whilst running errands. Marshall may have more personal hygiene than most pigs, but he still couldn't resist wallowing in a good mud bath when he saw one.

May pretended not to hear her. 'Ok, it's showtime.'

May rapped her ring-bejewelled fingers on the front door of the quaint cottage just a stone's throw away from the village green. Brightly coloured begonias lined the pathway up to the house - although some were just frayed stalks as if something had bitten the heads clean off. Marshall was here.

Within seconds, the door swung open to reveal Mrs Hoodwinkle in a mulberry coloured woollen skirt and matching jacket, with a floral frilled blouse sprouting out between the lapels. Her hair was perfectly preened and pinned with a pearl clasp, which matched her large pearl earrings.

'Oh, Ms Marvel! What a…pleasure,' she said insincerely. 'How can I help you?' Mrs Hoodwinkle was immaculately neat and tidy in appearance but the expression on her face was completely flustered.

'I hope I haven't caught you at a bad time!' May tried not to let her nerves make her voice waver. 'I've started a home delivery service and thought you would like your prescription of Snore Buns a week early this month?'

Cecelia Hoodwinkle's eyes widened with embarrassment as she poked her head out the doorway and glanced either side of the house to see if anyone was in listening distance.

'Oh, well I suppose that's alright, please won't you come in?' The lady of the house hurried May in with her shopping caddy, which accidentally got caught on the door frame and tumbled over into the hallway.

A muffled 'oomf' sounded from the caddy, which May quickly tried to drown out by coughing.

'C*eeeurrghhhceurrgggghghhh*! High pollen count today…' May bluffed.

May bent down to hoist the caddy back upright but Mrs Hoodwinkle got there first. 'Lucifer's hoof, that's heavy, Ms Marvel! How many home deliveries are you doing today?'

'Just a few! It's those Lose-a-Pound Cakes, they're a little dense, ironically, but nothing I can't handle!

Do let me take it, dear, you're dressed so lovely and smart I wouldn't want you to ruffle yourself up because of my clumsiness!' May barged Mrs Hoodwinkle out the way with her sizeable behind to block her view of the caddy whilst Aud passed her a paper bag of Snore Buns she was holding at the ready. Still reeling from May's compliment, Mrs Hoodwinkle had begun to admire herself in the hallway mirror, licking her finger and sticking a stray hair back into her bouffant. 'I'm due to meet with the council in just a moment, so if we could speed this up, yes?'

May started to flap as Aud still needed to search the house for Marshall, and Cecelia was about to throw them both out onto the doorstep.

Aud's scraggy hand surfaced from the caddy holding a vial of green liquid that unfortunately May had seen before. She swiftly snatched it from Aud's grasp and sneakily tapped a couple of drops into a china teacup sitting on the counter top that still had a slurp of Mrs Hoodwinkle's peppermint tea left inside it. Despite May's usual disapproval of Aud's concoctions, this time she had come up trumps.

'Won't you finish your tea, deary?' May took the teacup and pushed it into Mrs Hoodwinkle's hands as she turned from the mirror. 'It's important to keep hydrated!' She sipped the tea suspiciously, not taking her eyes off May, clearly losing patience with her visit.

'So, er, I don't suppose I can interest you in some of

my other products, can I, Councillor?'

Cecelia sipped the last of her tea and sighed in frustration. 'Listen, Ms Marvel, I appreciate you bringing round my…prescription. However, I really must ask you to leave-' The woman stopped mid-sentence and her eyes suddenly twinkled the colour green.

May stood holding her breath to find out whether the potion had worked or that they'd been discovered. Mrs Hoodwinkle's brow relaxed out of its frown and her eyes sparkled with interest. 'Yes, as I was saying! I really must ask you to leave me a list of your products!' Mrs Hoodwinkle seemed to be surprised with what she was saying, like someone had put the words into her mouth.

'In fact, I wouldn't mind trying a few samples!' Mrs Hoodwinkle made for the shopping caddy. It seemed that May had slipped the lady councillor a little too much Sweet-Talk Tonic, and she was more keen than May would have liked. It was one thing trying to convince her to buy some extra Snore Buns and a handful of Maca-Runes but it would be harder to talk her way out of why she was smuggling an elderly witch in a balaclava into her kitchen without getting a little suspicious.

'Wait!!' May roared, startling Mrs Hoodwinkle.

'Could I trouble you for a cup of tea?' Cecelia held May's gaze for a moment, then broke into a smile.

'Oh, but of course! You look positively withered with thirst, how rude of me.' May exhaled with relief, although couldn't help but wonder how withered she actually looked.

The pristine woman tottered off towards the kitchen to brew a pot of tea, having forgotten all about her meeting with the council. As she clattered and clinked around the kitchen, Aud took this as her chance to escape the confines of the trolley. As Mrs Hoodwinkle's back was turned, Aud emerged like a spider out of a plughole, one long leg at a time, and slunk out of the room with surprising stealth.

Mrs Hoodwinkle could only be hoodwinked for so long so Aud needed to pick up the pace. Meanwhile, May tried to keep Prudence's mother talking and glanced around the room to find a conversation starter. A family portrait was hanging on the wall in the hallway.

A stout, burly looking man stood proudly behind Mrs Hoodwinkle with his hand on her shoulder. She was sitting on a leather armchair and Prudence, although a couple of years younger on the photograph, was standing by her side. You could tell that Prudence took after her father - they had the same ruddy complexion and sour look on their faces like they'd both shared a grapefruit for breakfast.

'How is your delightful little daughter these days? What's her name, again? Primrose? Peaches?' May asked with false curiosity.

Mrs Hoodwinkle looked blank for a moment until May nodded toward the family portrait as a prompt.

'Oh! Of course, how silly of me! Yes, Prudy's quite

well, although acting a little odd these days. Normally all I hear is "I want," "get me this" and "buy me a new cat, I sat on it again" but some days all I can get out of her is a grunt. The other day I heard her rooting around in the fridge and so I told her to slow down on the pie and she snorted at me!'

May suspected that she hadn't been snorted at by her daughter at all, but in fact by Marshall. He was particularly partial to pie. May couldn't help but feel a little sorry for Prudence - her mother obviously didn't pay enough attention to her daughter to realise she was actually talking to a pig.

Mrs Hoodwinkle continued to stir the pot of tea she was still making, although it had brewed for so long that it looked like treacle. 'I'll bet it's the influence of those Wretcher children she's been hanging around with lately. Positively feral those two are, and now they're corrupting my lovely Prudy! You would think their parents would be ashamed of them, seeing as their father is a fellow council member. My little Pru is even beginning to smell like them now, it's like she's rolled around in a pig sty!'

May now had no doubt that Marshall was held up in this house somewhere. That was his signature scent. Aud was slithering about upstairs dressed in a knitted all-black ensemble, wrapping herself around every corner like a shadow. Usually Aud was as subtle as an elephant in dungarees, but when it came to espionage she was like a ninja.

Aud's quite large ears twitched when she heard

something coming from the room at the end of the hallway. She crouched down so that she was on her hands and knees and her joints crunched like a fortune cookie. She crawled along the floor until she reached the room where the noise was coming from. She had to rely on her ears because her knitted balaclava was beginning to bag a little so her nose started to poke through one of the eye holes.

As she peeked around the doorway, she could make out a rounded figure through the wool, rummaging through a chest of drawers. Aud grimaced as she saw poor Marshall in a blonde ringlet wig, a pink pinafore and frilly bloomers that poked out from under the dress as he truffled around in the drawer.

'Don't worry, my pot-bellied friend…' Aud mumbled

under her breath, 'I'll rescue you from this pink prison!' Aud pulled out a metal tube from her left nostril and a small dart out of her right one. It seemed that there were no bounds as to what she stored in that hooter of hers.

She slipped the dart in the tube and aimed for Marshall's bloomered buttock. 'Snore soundly, snorter…' She drew a deep breath and blew the dart and it pricked into his bottom like a pin into a marshmallow. He squealed on the dart's impact and crumpled to the ground.

She hooked the net over the unconscious frilly lump, hurled it over her shoulder and lumbered out of the bedroom. You would think that Aud didn't look like the strongest witch, but you'd be wrong! Aud did pilates everyday and had built up the core strength of a trapeze artist. But also, the net had been charmed to make the contents weightless - Aud had her arthritis to consider, after all.

As the witch tiptoed carefully down the staircase,

she could hear May struggling to keep the conversation going as the Sweet-Talk Tonic was beginning to wear off. Mrs Hoodwinkle had started to sound impatient again. May caught sight of Aud at the bottom of the stairs, signalling to the net and miming the pre-prepared phrase, 'the ham is in the hamper'. Mrs Hoodwinkle noticed that May's gaze had wandered over her shoulder, so she began to turn to see what had distracted her. May threw her arms around Mrs Hoodwinkle's shoulders in an embrace and kept a tight grip until Aud had successfully made her escape.

'Ms Marvel, please! Control your emotions!' Cecelia spoke with a squeak in her voice as May was cutting off her air supply.

'Thank you *so* much for having me, Councillor!' Mrs Hoodwinkle wriggled from May's grip and pushed her away to catch her breath. 'Now really, Ms Marvel! That's quite enough!' By now, Aud had managed to slip out unnoticed.

'Until next time, my dear! Ta ta!' And with a wave of her gold nail-polished fingers, May flew out the door with her caddy clattering behind her.

'Thank goodness! I thought she'd never leave.' Mrs Hoodwinkle straightened herself up in the mirror and flinched at the sound of someone munching away in the refrigerator. 'Oh, Prudy, at least *try* and eat like a lady.'

Snort.

Chapter Twelve

Marshall's rescue party crashed through the gingerbread door and fell in a heap on the floor. The sweet smell of the house made the contents of the net stir and groan - the sugary spice of the gingerbread roused the netted lump which started to try and kick its way out of the knitted trap.

'Let my poor baby out, Aud! My sweet boy can't breath!' May scrambled about on the floor trying to find the opening to the net.

'Calm down, darling, it's breathable cotton waffle weave!' Aud said impatiently. She spotted Marshall's curly tail poking through, so gave it a firm tug to coax him out.

'Aaarrgggh!!' a girlish voice shrieked, 'Stop pulling my hair!'

May and Aud froze on the spot before a look of dread washed across their faces. May turned to Aud, 'What did you do?'

Prudence clawed her way out of the net and staggered to her feet before going rigid the moment she saw May and a ferocious looking Aud towering over her. Prudence's bottom lip began to tremble in fear.

'Please don't hurt me! I'll do anything! I'm sorry I stole your stupid pig, ok?! But *please* don't tell my mother! And *please* don't bake me into a pie!'

May and Aud exchanged glances. May was frankly surprised at Prudence's reaction.

Aud stood scowling at Prudence, 'Give us one good

reason why we shouldn't, you little slug?' The

frightening woman reached into her cavernous nostril

and pulled out a rolling pin. May couldn't work out

whether she carried it around for self-defence or just in case she needed to make some emergency pastry. Aud threateningly slapped it against her palm which made Prudence whimper nervously.

'Oh, do stop it!' May confiscated Aud's weapon of mass dough-struction. 'Nobody's being made into a pie! You've read too many fairytales, girl! And *you* should know better!' she said as she shook the rolling pin shamefully at Aud.

Prudence breathed a sigh of relief. 'But that doesn't mean to say that you're off the hook, missy!' May continued, 'You can't just go around stealing other people's pigs, you know!'

Even though May wanted nothing more than to unleash her unbridled rage upon the little brat, she took a calming breath and took pity on the girl. 'Now, come on, we need to sort this mess out,' May said as she ushered the girl out the door.

May and Aud frog-marched Prudence back to her house to retrieve Marshall and to set the record straight with Prudence's mother. They all charged up the flowerless pathway but all collided into the front door like dominos as it was locked tight.

'Hellooo? Anybody hoooome?' May hollered through the letterbox, panic growing in her voice. 'Marshall, my love? Can you hear me? Come to Mamaaaaa! Where could they be? We were only just here! My poor boy, he must be terribly homesick. He probably hasn't eaten properly in days!'

'I wouldn't worry too much, May, sweetie.' Aud

pointed towards the garden gate, revealing a pile of rubbish littering the road ahead.

'Urgh, it stinks!' Prudence grimaced, pinching her nose. 'Looks like the foxes have got into the bins again.'

'I specifically said no junk food, the little swine! It gives him terrible digestive issues,' May despaired. Aud turned around to look at Prudence who had sat on the doorstep and started to cry. Aud had no time for weepers, 'Well, there's no point in sitting there boo-hoo-ing, girl! No one ever got anywhere by crying!' Prudence could hardly speak through blubbering breaths.

'At least you care about your, your, your, stupid p-p-pig, my mother hasn't even noticed I'm gooone!'

Aud cringed at the insufferable noise the girl was making.

'She never gives me any attention, all she cares about is her reputation! She's always volunteering for the council, she never wants to spend time with me-hee-heeeeee!' She wailed so pathetically until her face turned as crimson as the begonias would have been before Marshall had eaten them all down to stumps.

Aud was running out of patience. 'Listen, girly. I didn't get to the age I am feeling sorry for myself, you hear me?'

'How old *are* you?' Prudence gazed up, watery-eyed, at the craggy woman hunching over her.

Aud replied without a beat. 'Sixty-two. Now, listen.'

May raised an eyebrow.

'All people want in life is to be noticed. Noticed and accepted. And sometimes we forget who we really are because we're trying so hard to fit in. And maybe that's what your mother's trying to do at that stuffy old council. So much so, that she's forgotten what's really important. You. You're not a bad kid, Winkle. You remind me a lot of myself when I was your age. Now, your mother and I have never seen eye to eye - in fact, she was a mean crafty little-'

'Ok, that's enough, Aud, dear!' May decided to weigh in on the pep talk before Aud lowered the tone. 'Prudence, I'm sure your mother loves you dearly, but behaving badly and abducting people's pets isn't the right way to get her attention. I think you need to tell her how you feel.' Prudence nodded through silent sobs. 'Now then, where could your mother have gone?'

Prudence wiped her sleeve across her nose. 'I think she has a meeting at the Town Hall this afternoon.'

'Of course! Didn't she say she had a council meeting? You know, before we spiced up her peppermint tea?' Aud smirked.

May had forgotten Aud had been folded up like origami in her shopping caddy during their conversation. 'Oh, I hope we're not too late.'

'Too late for what?' Prudence snivelled.

'Pure chaos is what! Your mother will go spare when she realises you're not there, and in front of the whole council no less! And Marshall doesn't do well in high pressure situations.'

'It's not like he's leading the meeting,' said Aud. 'Stop getting your bloomers in a bunch.'

'No! What I mean is, he's had all that rubbish to eat which makes him terribly gassy. He could blow like my Great Aunt Flo's girdle when she's had gluten! Have you brought your broom, Aud?'

'No, I'm having it re-sanded. I got fed up of tweezing splinters out of my caboose.' Aud rubbed her buttock and winced.

'My mum has a Broomba?' Prudence suggested.

May snapped crossly, 'Not for cleaning, girl! For flying! We need to get to the town hall lickety-split!'

'She may be on to something, you know…' The rusty cogs in Aud's brain squeaked and creaked as she twiddled the hairs on her chin. 'I think I have an idea!' Aud plucked a hair pin out of her beehive, screwed one eye shut and started tinkering around in the keyhole. 'And you said I'd never use my lock-picking skills again.'

May corrected her, 'No, I believe I said you *should* never use them again, dear, but I'll turn a blind eye on this occasion.'

CLUNK. 'Bingo.'

Chapter Thirteen

Meanwhile, Mrs Hoodwinkle had arrived at Charlatan Town Hall. She hurried up the path towards the entrance with Marshall trundling behind her.

'Oh, stop dawdling, Pru!' She tugged at a ruffle on Marshall's dress in an attempt to shimmy her 'daughter' along. The pig let out a sad sigh as he'd developed a stomach ache halfway across Whispering Wood. May had always warned him about eating rubbish, but the delicious stench of a fresh compost bin was more than a pig could bear!

'You could have had a bath this morning, dear. You seem to have a certain aroma about you.' Cecelia wrinkled her nose at the smell, but she hadn't lifted her eyes from her notes the entire time she was talking to 'Prudence'.

'I hope you're not taking a leaf from the book of those ghastly Wretcher children. I don't know what their parents are thinking. I've heard they're a bit liberal with their parenting methods, but good grief, they let those two rule the roost! They let them get away with anything - and I'll eat my best hat if I let you go the same way.'

Marshall stood with a bemused expression, wondering what hats tasted like. All he could think about was his griping belly which had started to make his eyes water and a small squeal came out.

'Oh, darling, don't be so dramatic. Come on now, trot along, we're going to be late. I like to get here early for a good seat but I couldn't get rid of that nuisance, May Marvel.' Marshall sneered at the woman's insult. Inside they were met with around twenty council members sat on chairs behind tables arranged in a horseshoe, with a podium to join it together. A few stragglers drifted in behind and they took their seats.

'Go sit at the back, Pru, darling. We shan't be too long. Oh, Councillor Wickleburn! Save that seat! I have a couple of issues I'd like to go over with you!' She pulled out a sizeable folder from her curiously tiny designer handbag and Councillor Wickleburn let out an exasperated sigh as Cecelia dropped it with a *thud* on the table in front of him. He gave a weak smile out of politeness.

Instead of making his escape like any normal victim

of pig-nap, Marshall instead followed his snout to the refreshments table that had been set up at the back of the room. Maybe a couple of sandwiches might soothe his sore stomach.

Meanwhile, May, Aud and Prudence buzzed along at moderate speed aloft Mrs Hoodwinkle's new Broomba; it was the latest in household cleaning and was also turning out to be a worthy mode of transport. With help from one of Aud's hijacking hexes, this little vacuuming and dusting aid was now motoring at thirty miles per hour through Vexatious Vale. It was called Vexatious Vale because it was the most inconvenient road in Charlatan - there were more potholes than there were verrucas on Aud's feet, but it was the quickest route, so they had to make do.

136

There wasn't much room on the Broomba. May had taken up most of the space on the dinner plate-sized platform whilst Prudence clung on to the back of her. Aud was being dragged along behind in May's caddy.

'Brace yourselves!' May screamed, at the sight of yet another crater in the road. They all leant to the right, then to the left and to the right again to guide the Broomba in and out of the minefield of holes. Prudence knew the journey well as her mother had dragged her to countless meetings over the years.

'Take a left!' she yelled through a mouthful of May's hair.

One of Aud's ostrich legs appeared from the caddy and she dug her wellington boot into the dirt road to spin it off kilter. The Broomba flew round the corner with such force that they all toppled off and their vehicle whirred down to a spluttering halt. 'Drat! I gave it too much welly!' cursed Aud.

'Well, never mind! We'll have to go the rest of the way on foot.' May led the way whilst Prudence wheeled Aud in the caddy, hot on her heels.

***

'Next on the agenda is ongoing environmental concerns - Mrs Hoodwinkle, any new business?'

'Ahem! Why, thank you, Councillor Wickleburn!' Cecelia Hoodwinkle sidled out of her seat and stood behind the podium to address the council members. 'As a matter of fact, I have a few issues to address.' She waved a manicured hand over her weighty folder and it flicked at least one hundred pages through before landing with a *SLAM* open at the right page. Marshall squeaked in fright, halfway through a cheese and pickle sandwich.

'Is that your daughter, Councillor Hoodwinkle?' Mr Wickleburn squinted to the back of the room, which made the other council members crane their necks around.

'Er, yes, Prudence. But she won't be any trouble. Anyway, as I was saying, we've had several reports of vandalism in the village, including numerous cases of damsons in distress throughout Whispering Wood…'

'Excuse me? Prudence Hoodwinkle is *your* daughter?' A tall, pompous looking man stood up out of his chair. He was wearing a purple pinstripe suit with a lime green bow tie. His dark brown hair was slicked back so smooth that it gleamed in the light like a shiny conker.

Cecelia looked over at the man who had interrupted her. The man was Richard Wretcher - father to Gert and Floyd.

'That girl has been getting my children in trouble at Squiffler's - they're always in detention and she seems to be the ringleader!' The man pointed towards the back of the room where Marshall had moved on to a plate of flapjacks.

Mrs Hoodwinkle's face dropped, mortified. Mr Wretcher continued, 'Your daughter is an incredibly bad influence on Gert and Floyd and she should be ashamed of herself!'

Mrs Hoodwinkle clambered down from the podium.

'I beg your pardon, Sir? How dare you accuse my little Prune pie of such a thing! If anything, it's your filthy monsters that are causing my daughter to get into mischief, not the other way around!'

Every council member was now sat in stunned silence watching the drama unfold. One had even conjured a bowl of popcorn which she was shovelling into her mouth by the handful.

'Well, let's ask her, shall we?' enquired Mr Wretcher, beckoning Marshall over. Marshall waddled towards everybody, but only because he could smell the popcorn.

'Pru, tell them it's not true. You wouldn't disgrace Mummy like that.' Mr Wretcher and Mrs Hoodwinkle were nose-to-nose, glaring at each other. They weren't even looking at Marshall. The councillor with the popcorn clicked her fingers and the microphone appeared hovering in front of Marshall as he stood in the middle of the horseshoe of councillors.

Without warning, a thunderous rumble started to build in Marshall's pork belly. It rose at an unforgiving pace before erupting forth.

'BLEUUUUUUUGHHHHHAARRGGHHHHHEEER RRRGGGGHHH!!!'

The most deafening belch echoed over the microphone. The vibration shook the floorboards so violently, it caused the bowl of popcorn to bounce off the table. May, Aud and the real Prudence hurtled through the front doors at that very moment. 'Looks like we're too late,' said Aud.

Marshall immediately felt sweet relief from his stomach ache. Plus, he had made more room for the popcorn which had spilt all over the floor. He started vacuuming up the carpet of popcorn, (who needs a Broomba?) and the moment he bent over, his bloomers burst a seam and his pink curly tail sprouted out.

Mrs Hoodwinkle screamed in horror. Councillor Wickleburn, clearly tired of these shenanigans, struck a hammer on the table to restore some order. 'Can someone *please* explain what's going on here?'

Mrs Hoodwinkle pointed a shaking finger at Marshall's bottom, 'That is *not* my daughter!'

'Then where *is* your daughter, Madam?' Wickleburn demanded.

'I'm here,' a small voice piped up behind May. Prudence stepped out into view.

Prudence's mother looked at her daughter, then at Marshall, then back to Prudence, her bottom lip quivering with confusion. 'Explain!' The word burst from her mouth in one sharp shriek.

'I...I...I'm sorry, Mummy. But...it's all the Wretchers' fault!' Aud cleared her throat in warning behind Prudence, and she immediately corrected herself.

'What I mean to say is, I only started hanging around with Gert and Floyd because you weren't paying attention to me. I thought if I started being bad then you'd notice. But you didn't! You didn't even notice that wasn't me!' Prudence said, pointing at Marshall.

Mrs Hoodwinkle flushed with embarrassment.

'It was my idea to steal Ms Marvel's pig. I was going to give him back, I promise!' Prudence shuffled nervously on the spot, looking at her feet.

'Oh, Prudence, I don't know what to say…' Mrs Hoodwinkle's voice softened. Mr Wretcher started once more, 'Well, *I* certainly know what to say! How dare you accuse my children of such things. Tell me, girl, what other things should you be held accountable for? Was it your idea to destroy the village green? All our prize flowers ravaged and turned to mulch because of your reckless behaviour? Not to mention the chaos that followed!'

Prudence hung her head in shame and nodded. 'When we enchanted the garden gnomes, we only meant for them to pull up the flowers, not start attacking the children...'

Mr Wretcher wasn't finished. 'And let me guess, was it *you* who poisoned the punch at the village fete so everyone who drank it couldn't stop squawking like chickens?'

Prudence looked confused. May shook her head at Aud who was trying to hold in her laughter. Marshall was thinking about dinner.

Aud tried to change the subject, 'Well, I'd hardly call it poisoned - but what's done is done, kids will be kids, blah blah blah. There was no real harm done! Plus it was pretty funny…'

'Kids? I think you'll find, Madam,' he paused to look Aud up and down, 'that it's only one child that should be held responsible for all this! My children shouldn't be tarred with the same brush - they were just being led on by this terror!'

'I beg to differ, Sir.' Lillian was sitting quietly amongst the collection of councillors and was waiting for her moment to intervene. She stood up and the microphone popped into existence in front of her.

'I happen to have incriminating video evidence of

these vandals at work, thanks to my newly installed Gnome Drones. After we'd managed to round up the rogue gnomes following the fete, we programmed them to act as surveillance for the village. They've been set up all over Charlatan - it was our next order of business in this meeting before all of this hullabaloo!'

Lillian continued, 'Not only was it set in place to identify the culprits but there's also been a handful of werewolf sightings. Thankfully the creature seems quite docile as there have been no attacks, but the village bakery bins keep getting ransacked every full moon - it makes a frightful mess!'

Mrs Hoodwinkle's eyes bulged in yet another horrific realisation of the day. She'd forgotten to eat her Snore

Bun prescription one night last month and she thought perhaps she'd got away with it.

Lillian turned to Mr Wretcher who had suddenly gone quiet, 'How sure *are* you, Sir, of your son and daughter's innocence before we play this footage in front of the council?'

Mr Wretcher turned pale. Cecelia had turned an inexplicable colour. In fact, she looked as if she would keel over. Mr Wretcher composed himself, 'I'm sure that won't be necessary. I think Mrs Hoodwinkle and I can come to some kind of arrangement as to what their punishment should be.'

Lillian winked at May.

'I believe I have a suggestion?' proposed May, with a twinkle in her eye.

Chapter Fourteen

Prudence ended up spending the summer giving pedicures to old pensioner witches: washing their warty feet, massaging their corns and buffing their bunions. If she managed to keep up her end of the deal, then May would agree to let Prudence help with her delivery service, and make a little pocket money on the side. Aud had also managed to pull a few strings at the familiar farm where she had spent most of her youth. She had made sure that Gert and Floyd would spend their summer shovelling and bagging up familiar fertiliser for the Charlatan Gardening Society.

Cecelia reduced her hours at the council in order to spend more quality time with her daughter. When Prudence had completed her community service, she and her mother began to take frequent trips to their holiday home in Greenbeak with their newly adopted familiar, Joan, the parrot.

Joan sat on Prudence's shoulder wherever she went and became a loving companion for the girl. Birds gave Aud the heebie-jeebies, even more so when Joan started to mimic Cecelia Hoodwinkle, wittering in Aud's ear whenever Prudence came round for her delivery duties.

Determined to make the best of a bad situation, Aud had taken pride in teaching Joan to chant *'Cecelia Squealer! Cecelia Squealer!'* - a nickname she'd coined for Prudence's mother when they were school girls at Saint Squiffler's on account of how often Cecelia tattled on Aud. From then on, Joan was made most welcome and had also become firm friends with Marshall.

Much to May's shame and Aud's delight, the local

newsletter had announced that May Marvel had won Best Baker for the tenth year in a row - a decade of triumphs! The two cronies had a celebratory gathering to mark the controversial occasion.

May invited Rose, Violet and Lillian, as well as Gareth and his new girlfriend, Minnie Mucus.

They ate Marshall's second favourite meal which was beef wellington (served in an actual wellington) just in case their new froggy friends were offended by toad in the hole.

Marshall emptied his wellington before eating the boot itself. He sighed contently before drifting off into a sleepy stupor dreaming of Snore Buns, popcorn and tomorrow's breakfast.

The End.